THROW BACK

My Love Towards Poetry

R. GANDHIMATHI

AKAVAI PUBLICATION

COPYRIGHTS

Mrs. R. Gandhimathi is a teacher and a poet. She has been writing professionally since 2020. She believes that poetry can change the world, and she uses it to inspire and empower young people through her writing. She promises to pull heart strings, offer laughs through her creative writing.

She is a regular contributor to Creative Writers group. She is the co-author for two anthology books "Priyamana Thozhi", "My Favourite Teacher" by Akavai Publication

She is working as a co-author for an upcoming anthology book "Bouquet of Emotions" by Creative Writers.

Preface

Poems shares feeling

Let my words be healing

Messages awakening

The aim of this book "Throw Back" collection of poems makes the reader to have a quick rewind of past memories. Readers can feel their journey of life. The verses are easy simple to understand and rich with in-depth concept to make the readers, easy reading and catch the different phases of life through poems.

I am much elated in presenting my first edition "Throw Back" with sub-title "My love towards poetry". It is shaped by deep thoughts with a feathery touch to so the elegant hearts of the readers.

Themes waves around the various stages of life such as and the people around. The readers school days can feel that their life is a collection of memories.

I am presenting a bouquet of my emotions to the readers. Let everyone feel their emotions with its ecstatic fragrance.

I assure that my poems will surely touch the readers, do welcome and encourage me in my future endeavors.

I record my sincere thanks to all those who are associated with the publication of my outputs literary.

R. Gandhimathi

Foreword

It gives me immense pleasure to write a foreword to the book "Throw Back" by Mrs. R. Gandhimathi. She is a successful teacher and a versatile teacher. All her poems are remarkable for their consistency and creativity. Some poems make the readers read again and again. Verses are powerful, motivating and commendable. I admire her flair for writing about the various topics in her unique style. All the topics are worth reading and mentoring. I wish to quote a few lines from her collections.

"Every thought is a spark; Spark makes you sharp"

"Life starts with a heartbeat; Ends with drum beat"

"Think every day is a blessing; Cross it without stressing"

"Life without dreams; Are cakes without creams"

"Live within your budget; You will not be upset"

"Life is an art; Learn to be smart"

Like these striking verses are scattered throughout the book tremendously. I am confident that her inspiring verses will enrich the spirit of readers and render a delightful experience. My hearty wishes to the poet for all her endeavors to come true in future.

Mr. M. Kasilingam

Physical Education Director

K.R.M Matric Hr. Sec. School

Perambur

FOREWORD

I am indeed happy to script a foreword to this awesome poetry collection **Thrown back** by Mrs. Gandhimathi. The preface itself gives a healing touch. It takes us to our own old reminiscence as there are so many good memories in our past journey of life. What we have to do is just recollect, poet Gandhimathi has done that. All the poems are simple and lucid in style for the readers to understand easily. They are rich in meaning. Her love towards poetry is immense. Let me tell a few words about her. In fact, we are travelling in the WhatsApp group of 'Creative Writers'. She is very sincere, dedicated and regular. We are very proud to see emerging poetess from our group.

We ourselves will become a child when we read the poems. For example, in the poem **Dad,** father is elevated to a greater height. The poem **Encourage,** encourages all. It inspires all the readers to be like a catalyst in others life.

Every beginning has an end is like a philosophical verse. It ends up to have a good hope and tells God is always with us. As human being we commit a lot of mistakes. Lovely lines we get from the verse **I think I like you.** When many of us feel so lonely and isolated this verse gives a bright light. How rightly it is said. Believe it or not, life is a mystery. **Nothing is too late and never give up** shows that we can achieve if we keep working.

The poet concludes the book with some interesting poems like **Smile keeps you going** and **spreading love then success and failure are a part of our life**.

I sincerely believe all the readers will enjoy this book and keep it as a treasure. May it reach many hands, may this book be read by many readers. I wish her all success.

D. BRINDA

GRADUATE TEACHER

GOVT HIGH SCHOOL,

MELPATTAMPAKKAM

CUDDALORE

FOREWORD

Mrs. Gandhimathi, PGT Teacher in Accountancy & Commerce has compiled poems on various aspects of life and nature and has used rhyming scheme so well which makes reading a pleasure. The collections of poems mostly dwells on confidence required to meet the challenges and uncertainty of life. It is understandable being a teacher she has devoted much of her focus to motivate and instil confidence in all her poems. It is evident that she is a great admirer of nature that her most of the poems sites nature for inspiration and never give up attitude.

Butterflies in Heart captures the vivid moments of love at first sight at description of little thinks bringing in unlimited happiness is titled as beauty. Crazy Moment of Life, Change in Life and Krishna in all these poems the author very beautifully expresses the precious gift of God a Child to a mother. Dad is a wonderful thought of gratitude so fondly recalled by a child.

Forget & Forgive reminds saintly poet Thiruvalluvar's saying to keep doing good and forget hurts. The author also describes the pain a person suffers because of misplaced faith and denied love. She also expresses values and importance of Friendship and lovely memories of school days in Friendship.

The author expresses what a smile can do as wonders and her message to spread love and empathy. She also fondly recollect what a dedicated teacher could contribute to a student and narrates the sacrifices of Women. On the whole on reading these collections of Poems of various topics the reader shall definitely draw inspiration, remain calm, approach challenges with smile and be compassionate to human beings and be a loving and caring person.

I wish the author and the reader the most pleasant experience of good literature.

M.S.Tholkappian B.Com., FCA., Grad.CWA.

Partner. M/S Dhandapani &Tholkappian, Chartered Accountants.

FOREWORD

Mrs. Gandhimathi is a budding poetess. She expresses her thoughts, emotions and feelings in a unique manner. Her style of writing is simply astonishing. This is a collection of so pretty sweet poems on the title, "Throw Back".

Inside every poem there is a deep feeling hidden which attracts all the readers.

Her concluding lines have a peculiar note to strive a different point to the readers.

I wish to quote a few striking lines from her poems.

Be a better thinker

No one can stop you becoming a winner

Born to win

Success is always possible

Until it's your last attempt

Encourage all

One day your life will shine

Make you fine

Give yourself time

Travel with ambition

Think you are the best edition

Life is uncertain

I wish this book will reach many readers to get inspiration and motivation

Mrs. PUSHPAVALLI RAVICHANDRAN

H. O. D.

English Department,

Kaligi Ranganathan Montford Matric. Hr. Sec. School,

Perambur,

Chennai - 11.

Butterflies in Heart

I saw my soul mate near a gate

I got carried away by his smile

I stood for a while

I couldn't take my eyes

My heart took a flight

At the first sight

I wanted to hold his hand tight

My heart beat faster

I became hot like a toaster

Active like a rooster

Ready to loot him like a gangster

With a change in my blood pressure

A sudden shake in my nervous system

I felt like losing myself

Butterflies in my heart

I got in to a fairy world

With lots of dreams

Born to win

Born to win

Earth do spin

Don't be inside a tin

Achieve before you go to coffin

Get out of your comfortness

Everything is possible with effortness

Use your smartness

Reach your highness

Every thought is a spark

Spark makes you sharp

Don't let your thoughts to park

Always fix a benchmark

Be a better thinker

No one can stop you becoming a winner

Banyan tree

Banyan tree represents endless life

It's a family tree

If you live like a banyan tree

Your life becomes glee

It stands majestically

Never worried about thunder

Withstands all hinder

One of the God's wonder

It acts as a healer

Don't behave like a business dealer

Who leads the life in a hurry

Without giving importance for any

You may be a winner

Behind you there is always a runner

If you have ability

Always there is a possibility

Beauty

Beauty of small things

A smile of a child

Drops of rain

Window seat of a train

Buzzing sound of a bee

Makes our life meaningful

Nature is always colorful

Earth is wonderful

Be merciful

Pet animals are faithful

Certain situations are painful

Resources are handful

Be little careful

Are you playful

Always be grateful

Life is always beautiful

Balloon

I sell colourful balloons

People go gazing at the balloons

Children get excited

They hop and scream

They come running to buy balloons

I am an instigator of life

Our life is like a balloon

Keep pouring good thoughts

Don't hold it too tight nor

Leave it in the air

Take control of your life

If not your life becomes out of control

I earn less money

I am one among the many

Who spread happiness

Still my life is colourless

Cock is the best clock

Cock a doodle do

A natural alarm of God

It's a morning call for all

The Sun slowly shows its face

And lights up the earth

Reminds me about the purpose of birth

All creatures are worth

And says happy morning all

The cock is the best clock

Which no one can block

It helps you to unlock

The surprises of God

Do your duty

Their lies the real beauty

Self-motivation is the best

You are the best

Never expect appreciation from the rest

Cock a doodle do

Child in me

I see, the sea

I could see a child in me

I start playing with sand

I become an engineer building castle

An instant happiness

Which makes me a billionaire

An unexpected rain

It relieves my pain

I start making paper boats

I become a helmsman

An instant happiness

That is unlimited

I see candy

I am always my dad's candy

He calls me honey

An instant happiness

I fly like an angel

Crazy Moments of Life

Crazy moments of life

First is always the best

As we are unaware about the next

First meet of my little hero

My lifetime treasure

It was my pleasure

To hold him in my arms

His first sight was a delight

I touched his little fingers

Smiled at his funny legs

Heart made little Jerks

Tears in my eyes

He was crying with fears

I hugged him and said

Welcome dear

I am here

To protect you forever

Dad

Worked hard to earn

Gave all comforts you can

You are my superman

Taught me life lessons as much you can

So that I could lead my life without fear

My teacher, motivator

The one and only best friend

Who always lived very simple

Spoke to everyone with words humble

Truthfulness was your symbol

Fought life with confidence

Shared all your experience

Never disturbed anyone till the end

From the depth of my heart

Dad I love you

But God got you

You left your little angel

It's ok ,You are(RK)

Happy heavenly Father's day

Dawn to dusk

Dawn to dusk

Decisions are a must

Be a divergent thinker

Decisions are thought process

One way a natural process

It is not a hard process

Still a step by step process

Deciding in advance is planning

Helps you to have a stress free living

Don't be afraid of risk taking

A success key for your earning

Sometimes results can be heart - breaking

Pains can help you in learning

Experience is the best teacher

Which no one can impart

Encourage all

Be a catalyst in other's life

Live with inspiration not with desperation

There is always time

Wait for your life to rhyme

Be like a seed

Motivating is a good deed

Hope is a protective shield

Days will come where you can reap a good yield

If you see a mist

Don't think life is worst

It's a period of rest

Understand the twist

Equip yourself with knowledge

Overcome the hurdles

There is nothing called Failure

Whatever you do is just an attempt

Success is always possible

Until it's your last attempt

Ego

Let it go Let it go

It is just your Ego

My soul said this long long ago

Your beauty lies in action

So work with passion

All you need is attention

To get perfection

Don't make complications

Compress your reactions

Have good intentions

Be humble

Your body is a temple

Let's make it simple

Don't be with pride

Wait for your tide

Nothing to hide

Just wait for your final ride

Every beginning has an end

Every beginning has an end

Think every day is a blessing

Cross it without stressing

Live your life as if there is no next day

Life is all about collection of moments

Always follow your inner voice

Ignore the noise

Face life without fear

Death is not near

Have hope

God is always with us

Forgive and forget

Trust is a must

If not life becomes the worst

Betrayal of trust

Makes my heart burst

Nervous system breaks

An unbearable pain

Unforgettable strain

You made a mist by giving a twist

Every lie made me die

I feel like a broken mirror

Though it's your error

You made me a fool, you act so cool

Wound is soo deep, I could not control my weep

Negative thoughts peep

Don't heap nothing you can reap

Life is not cheap

Scars left cannot be left

Still I have right to correct and forgive

Follow me

Follow your intuition

There is nothing called life definition

Each has their way of recognition

Never have rigid composition

Life is not all about competition

Have your own ambition

If necessary go for transformation

You will be able to achieve your mission

Flow like a river

Flow like a river

There is nothing to shiver

Learn to be a good swimmer

Break your pessimistic thoughts with a hammer

Be a reason

Don't change yourself like a season

Jade never fades

Run like a horse

As if there is no recourse

Of course life has no special course

Learn it by your experience

Give yourself time

Give yourself time

One day your life will shine

Make you fine

Get out of your cocoon

Spread your wings

Fly, fly until you reach your destiny

Never lose your will power

It's the only way to empower

Give yourself a space

You are not in a race

Don't try to chase

Pick your pace

Life is like a maze

Which will make you amaze

Let's overcome by God's Grace

It changed my life

It changed my life

A memorable moment

When I saw my little one

Immediate shower from my eyes

Nothing I could do much

Just a face to face touch

Felt the warmth

Pain stopped just like a rain

Power I could regain

Learnt how to be patient

Hours passed like minutes

One thing I understood

Life is valuable

Memory is the only thing we could carry

What a Blessing

The Biggest surprise of God

My life - time gift

If I Get Wings

If I get wings

Confidence it brings

Let your dreams fly

Which no one can tie

Try to find a heart which never lie

Overcome the hinder

Without any blunder

Reach your destination

With enthusiasm

A sense of freedom

Helps you to acquire wisdom

Easy to tackle the problem

New thoughts blossom

Life looks awesome

I think I like you

I think I like you

Reasons are many

Let me tell you honey

You are handsome

Your humour sense is awesome

You make me blossom

When you are near

There is no fear

A feel of getting a feather

Flying high in all-weather

Like a sun you are bright

Like a night you are quiet

Furious like a sea

This makes me curious to see

You sound like a trumpet

Trained me like a parrot

King of my chariot

I Remember

The day when my love got devastated

The pain which I never tasted

A gift for true love

I was left alone

An unknown fear in my heart

As if I got hit by a dart

Darkness around me

I couldn't breathe

My life dreams got buried

But my sweet heart was never worried

I Cried, screamed, groaned

No one was around to wipe my tears

It took lot of years

To come out of treachery

Still stays as an injury

Inner voice

Everybody listen

Our life is a lesson

Looking for fusion

Getting adapted to the latest fashion

God is the planner of our life

Are you concerned about material possession

Worrying about the missed session

Always having comparison

Earning without intermission

Looking for recognition

Life is surrounded by competition

Always dreaming about achieving high position

Attracted towards imitation

What is the use of our long vision

When God has already written your mission

God is a mathematician

He will lead you to your destination

King of my heart

My king

My lander,

My Enchanter

Master of my heart

Block buster

You are a storm

Still calm

A big surprise of God

I am blessed

You are my mine

Rain or shine

You made be fine

You are a maze

You made me go craze

All happened by God's Grace

Life is uncertain

Life is uncertain

Try to make it certain

Are you searching for a lantern?

Follow your own pattern

The sweetness of life is hidden

Explore to make it happen

Miracles are sudden

Heart teaches us life lesson

Kindly try to listen

Heart beats until the end of its mission

Are you ready for your expedition?

Travel with ambition

Think you are the best edition

Give importance to your composition

I Believe, God is the best magician

Lesson from trees

Trees teach us a valuable lesson

Let's us all listen

Trees shed leaves to refresh

Let go your past to live your present

Trees withstand all seasons

Try to overcome all situations

Life is full of changes

Tree is a symbol of patience

Give without expectation

No discrimination

Don't expect appreciation

Show Gratitude

Be with good attitude

Don't be a fool

Be cool

Plant trees and save environment

Life without dreams

Life without dreams

Are cakes without creams

Birds without feathers

I dream, I scream

I smile

I run what a fun

I cry without being shy

A fear as if nothing is near

I could see, I could hear

What a reel, make a deal

A fantastic feel

Which no one can give

I am the Director

I am the heroine

Of the film named Dreams

A story which never ends

Eagerly waiting for the next show

Every script has a great flow

Life is an art

Life is an art

Learn to be smart

Is life a shopping mart?

To buy everything as you want

Earth is a fantastic tourist spot

Enjoy every second of your travel

Never feel bad about you

Are you panic?

Confidence is your tonic

Always have an optimistic thought

Happiness and Sorrow are part of life

Seed or weed, you can definitely do your best

Take decisions as per your intuition

Get ready to leave your impression

Well we are all God's creations

Never give up

Never give up

The beginning is tough

Life path is not always rough

Don't be a blert

Sometimes words hurt

To have a happy life, you need to be alert

Think I can do

If not no one can do

Self-confidence is a must

Obstacles only can bring your best

Problems are like a test

Solutions may have a twist

Nature is the best teacher

It helps you to get your good feature

Be an achiever

Nothing is too late

Nothing is too late

Unless you hate

Don't try to rate

Never say it's my fate

Fear to eliminate

Confidence is there to illuminate

If you Isolate

People around you will manipulate

Your mind may bifurcate

Never lose hope

You may be a slow walker

Don't stop

Until you go to the top

Nothing can flop

If you are smart

Nothing is too late

Definitely everyone has a special day

It can be any day

Keep working

Make life colourful

Make life colourful

Let's be cheerful

Do activities to make life wonderful

Go for adventures which give you thrill

Engage yourself in creating new things

It helps you to come out of mood swings

Every poem gives me wings

Lot of glee it brings

If you are empty, your thought shrinks

Experiment whatever your heart say

Life is a bay, focus like a ray

Think every moment is a blessing

Nothing should be missing

My Krishna

You made us wait for years

My dear Little Krishna

His first smile

Got stored in my memory file

It is a jiggle

My life's wriggle

His first step

Gave me a pep

He is naughty

Still he is my beauty

He is an unlimited edition

With lot of petition

He is adamant

To get what he has determined

He updates his mischief

Wipes my tears with kerchief

Life cycle is a mystery

Life cycle is a mystery

Definitely you can achieve victory

Every human passes through different phases of life

Life is full of trial and error analysis

Try to gain experiences as much as you can

This is what you are going to carry till your end

Experience is the true teacher

Memories are recorded in our brain

Which no one can drain

Confidence always helps you to regain

Look at the nature

Do they complain

They simply wait for the next season

Solve the puzzle in your own style

Puzzles do have more than one solution

Are you waiting to find a reason?

Only time can give you the answer

That you have missed to live your life

Life is peaceful

Life is peaceful

When you are grateful

Don't take everything to your heart

Pain is just a part

Try to keep negatives apart

Get over your emotions

Nothing stays with us till our end

Everyone is special

Never peep in to others life

Artificial sweetener always taste good

Caution not to be carried away

Change your mindset

Live within your budget

You will not be upset

It's the time to get set

Life does not have the option of insert

Live your life with peace

Not as a broken piece

Love loses its value

Love loses its value

When it is given to a wrong person

Who never tries to understand

Not even given a space in their heart

Pretend to be a good heart

But leave us in drought

People play in such a way

They make us feel guilty

Push us to a situation which is empty

They will not understand the damages

No regret about their behaviour

Better try to be a donor

You can get honour

Give without expectation

There lies your satisfaction

If you expect perfection,

You will end up with frustration

Lesson from my life

Lesson from my life

Life without a penny

Teaches you many

People look at you funny

Even your Honey

Looks for money

Are you crazy behind money

Nothing comes with you honey

Twist and turns in life

But no one can return your life

something lost never comes back

No real hearts I could find

Without knowing this

I was chasing my love

Expecting to live like a dove

If you have invited a problem

Only time can give you a solution

Don't feel, no one to deal

It's your life

Lessons are the valuable gifts of life

Our friendship is

Our friendship is divine

Until we remain

Friend is like a mirror

Helps you to travel without an error

A relationship which we can select

Which accepts our defect

Love without side effect

You can be thyself

Life is a journey

Friend is the only person

Who travels without expectation

A person who never hates

Rather he waits

Never changes with trend

A friend is a friend till your end

Positivity

Very morning is a sign of positivity

Smile increases your longevity

Imagination leads to creativity

Learning enhances your ability

Throw away the negativity

Trying to find the opportunity

Come out of ambiguity

Kindness gives credibility

Always live with integrity

Rhythm of life

Music is the rhythm of life

Feel the music

It is always classic

The first beat is the heart beat

Which no musician can beat

My nightingale is my mother

Music creates bonding

Lasts till our ending

Nature is the best musician

Birds are the best singers

Animal's sounds are unbeatable

They create tunes on their own

Which are unknown

No music director, lyricist

Yet a music feast

Nature does not rest

Until it does its best

Music gives us energy

Which helps us to live with synergy

Son

My Hero

You are my wonder

You laugh like a thunder

Like a commander

You made me surrender

You are my treasure

It's my pleasure

I forget my pressure

I run without leisure

You are my shower

It gives me power

You are my happiness

You are my sunshine

You are my twinkle

You are my soul

You are my Hero

School days

School days are golden days

Memories are like fresh flowers

Thoughts flow like rivers

Friends are our world

Brain was our only gadget

Life had meaning without earning

We were happy even without a penny

Enjoyed summer with humour

Never searched for an umbrella

Made paper boats

Wet or sweat our fun was unlimited

Touched fire without fear

Took everything at ease

Friends made me to run to make fun

Hunger never gave anger

Birthdays were great days

Enjoyed festivals at great levels

Summer holidays in granny's house

All days were special

Years went with excitement and fun

Silence is the best answer

Silence is the best answer

In life try to be an Eraser

Rather than pointing out others

No one is a perfect master

When you are hurt be silent

Don't be violent

Smile and let it go

If someone ignores

Don't handle with arrogance

Think about their ignorance

Be patient, give them a chance

Time will change

So that everyone knows your range

Teacher

My favorite teacher

He always thought about student's future

A good observer

Met with an accident and lost his right hand

He practised to write with left hand

Always wore a shirt with full hand

Still he was our right hand

His life was our inspiration

He helped us in Board Exam preparation

A real example of determination

Wake up dear

Wake up dear

Sunrise is near

Work hard without fear

Flow like a river

Success is beside you forever

Reflect like a mirror

Make a society without an error

Live with determination

Not with discrimination

Life seems to be mysterious

If you are superstitious

Be ambitious

Never be bilious

Don't forget life is precious

Get out of your darkness

It's time, wakeup dear

When I meet you I'll

Friends forever

Promised to stay with me forever

Though you are not near

Memories stays with me forever

You are my blood vessel

The one who made all my days special

Life was a bliss

Without you a miss

You made me empty

Though I am blessed with plenty

I wish to meet you, my friend

Years have rolled without you

Let me hold your hand

Shall we go for a round

Surprise me with a rose

Looking for your shoulder

You are my beholder

May God grant you, his blessing

When all my plans fail

When all my plans fail

Believe me

God has already made a big plan for you

Learn to take things easy

Never be lazy

Life cannot be always cozy

Sometimes it is little shaky

Life seems to be tricky

You can be more happy

If you are not choosy

Accept the fall

Recover from the troll

Problems are always small

Think only about the solutions

Don't get carried away by illusions

Women's heart is an ocean

Women's heart is an ocean

Changes with reason

Varies like season

She lives her life with passion

The mother of patience

Try to show your affection

Women are like cool breeze

Don't take them for ease

She is strong by heart

To understand her is an art

So be smart

She plays different roles

She is a gale

A Phoenix Bird

Her endless love drives you mad

Don't make her sad

She is your rib

Treat her with equity

What is life???

What is life???

Life starts with a heartbeat

Ends with drum beat

It is a blessing

Don't give more attention

To what is missing

Are you trying to do editing?

Your fate is already written

So try your level best to fit in

God is the Director of our life

He decides the role for you

Every one is blessed with skill

If you are chill

You can enjoy the thrill

Life is not a treadmill

Get down so that you can fill

The gap between the beat and the drum

Smile keeps you going

Smile keeps you going

Secret which is unknowing

Smile is a positive vibe

Which helps you to live your life

A gift for humans

Which no other creatures has

Enjoy the taste of life

It is the best medicine of hope

Everyone has to face his / her tough days

Think about your best days

Look for different ways

Overcome the hindrance with a smile

As these are our memorable days

Which stays in our heart as unforgettable days

Keep smiling

Have a long life

Spread love

Spread love

I wonder how

Just a smile you show

Makes others wow !

Empathy is the need of hour

If you inculcate, blessings will shower

Love flows like a river

For everlasting relationship it's a power

Actions are love triggers

People who care

Are now a days rare

Teach the younger generation about sharing

Importance of caring

To do charity without disparity

Tell them what you do today

Will be rewarded back double tomorrow

Spread love like a bird

Success and failure are part of life

Happy about winning

Are you upset about Losing?

Winning is a bliss

Failure is just a miss

Stop chasing

Life is all about living

Enjoy the happening around

Wait for the sunshine

Until then help others to be fine

Life is soo special

Everyone has got his / her potential

Morals are essential

Try to be like a honey bee

Though it passes through lot of obstacles

It searches only for goodness

Acknowledgement

My dreams of penning poems have been come true with a ray of hope from the "Creative Writers" group. I wish to surrender my whole hearted gratitude to Mrs. D. Brinda Srinivas for shaping me as a writer.

I would like to pay my special regards to Mrs. Pushapavalli for her fantastic editing and appreciation which decorates as a crown to my book.

I wish to submit my sincere thanks to Mr. Tholkappian for rendering a harmonious forward.

I wish to submit my sincere thanks to Mr. Kasilingam for his hearty foreword and encouragement.

This project would not have been possible without my companions of "Creative Writers" Family. Their reviews, appreciation means a lot.

Finally, I should appreciate the help of Mr. Barathwaj, Computer Assistant, who worked without time limits and my publisher, who guided and supported me in bringing out this book successfully.

I want to thank God, without his blessing this wouldn't be possible.